For my family

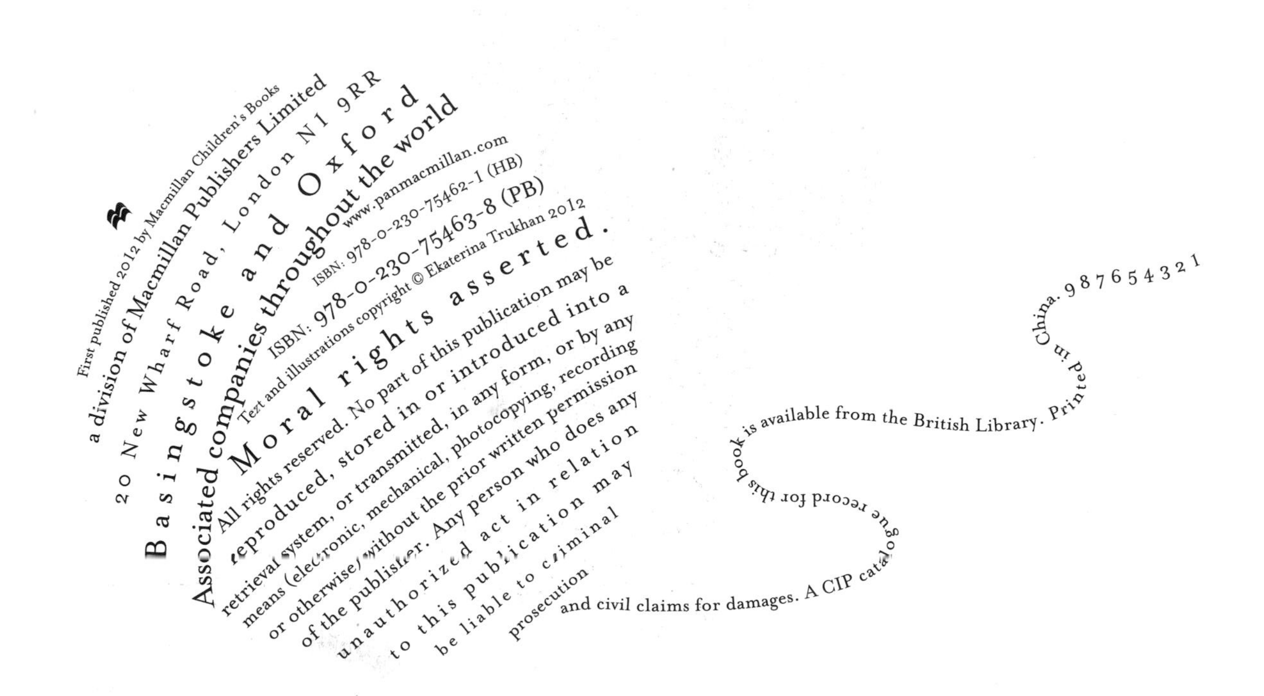
First published 2012 by Macmillan Children's Books
a division of Macmillan Publishers Limited
20 New Wharf Road, London N1 9RR
Basingstoke and Oxford
Associated companies throughout the world
www.panmacmillan.com
ISBN: 978-0-230-75462-1 (HB)
ISBN: 978-0-230-75463-8 (PB)

A CIP catalogue record for this book is available from the British Library. Printed in China. 9 8 7 6 5 4 3 2 1

EKATERINA TRUKHAN

ME AND MY CAT

MACMILLAN CHILDREN'S BOOKS

This is me...

and this is my cat!

We're the best of friends, and
we spend all our time together.

We play inside,

and outside.

We love to race and chase,
but my cat's always
too fast for me!

He gets into lots of places I can't.

And into some places he shouldn't!

WOOF WOOF

But whenever he needs me,

MEOW!
I'm always there to help.

And if I ever need a little help . . .

. . . my cat races straight to my rescue too.

Because that's what best friends do.

At dinner-time,
me and my cat
like to relax
together with a
tasty snack.

When my cat has
finished his dinner . . .

. . . he always helps me finish mine!

After a long day playing, I like to wash and splash in a bubbly bath. But my cat doesn't.

He prefers to wash himself,

far away from any bubbles!

At bedtime, we cuddle up close and read our favourite story.

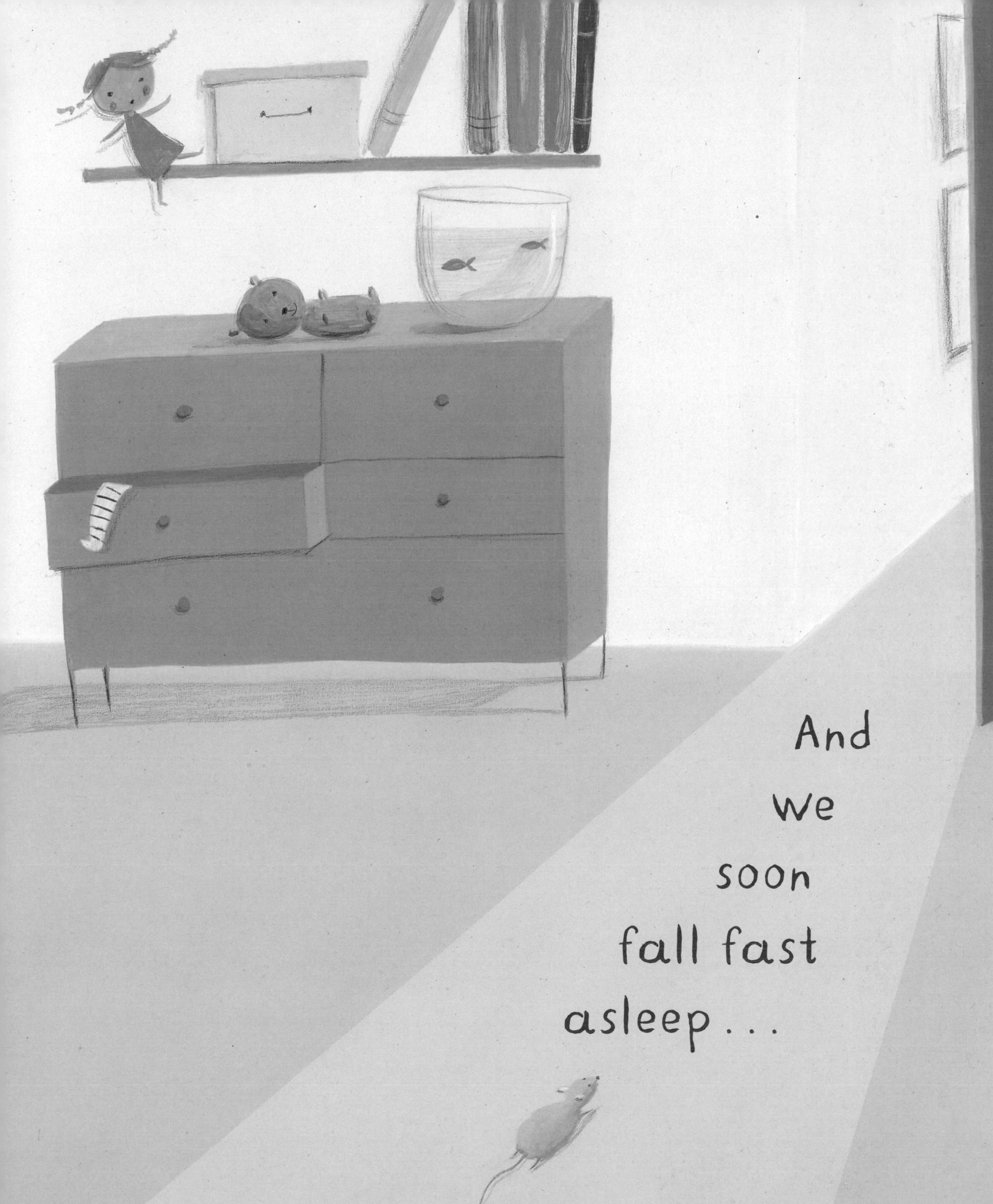

And
we
soon
fall fast
asleep . . .

Just me...

z z Z Z Z

and my cat.